W9-ASA-111

SARAH'S ROOM

SARAH'S ROOM

by Doris Orgel

WITH PICTURES BY

Maurice Sendak

HARPER COLLINS PUBLISHERS
NEW YORK

Library of Congress catalog card number: 63-13675

For Ernst Adelberg

On Sarah's wall, green trees grow tall,
and morning glories bloom.
Of all the rooms in all the world,
the best is Sarah's room.

On Jenny's wall, no trees at all
can grow, no blossoms bloom,
for Mother won't put paper on
the walls in Jenny's room.

When Jen was small,
    she marked her wall,
with smudges and with smears.
Wallpaper would be wasted there,
that is what Mother fears.

Sarah sweeps and keeps her room
clean all by herself.
She has some small glass animals
in rows upon a shelf.

Under Sarah's window stands
a dollhouse painted white.
It has a bell that really rings,
and an electric light.

One day, while Sarah was away,
Jen came, on muddy feet,
and left some mud on Sarah's floor
that always looked so neat,

And muddied up the wallpaper,
and tore a doll's best dress,
and turned the dollhouse inside out,
and made an awful mess!

That's why they put a latch up high
on Sarah's door. Oh, when
will Jenny ever get to go
into that room again?

"I wish I may, I wish I might,"
Jen wishes on a star
that someday sister Sarah
would leave her door ajar.

The starlight gleams
    while Jenny dreams,
and then it seems to say:
"You can reach that little latch,
you can go in and play!"

"I'll catch you, latch! I'll reach you!"
says Jen, and dreams some more:
Look, she pulls the hook out,
she opens Sarah's door!

The dollhouse light is bright that night.
The dollhouse children call:
"Jenny, come inside our house,
it's not too small at all!"

Jenny stays and plays with them.
They show her all their things—
their beds and books and all their toys—
and then the mother brings

Refreshments on a little tray.
Jen has a lollipop,
and whipped-cream cake, and wishes
the dream would never stop.

"Oh, Jenny, stay, don't go away!"
the dollhouse children cry.
"No," Jenny tells them. She must go,
and kisses them good-bye.

From way up high, Jen hears a sigh,
a soft and sad "Alas!"
Up on the shelf, the tiny cow,
that's made of shiny glass,

Says with a *moo*, "I beg of you,
bring me a blade of grass,
for that is what I long to chew,
although I'm made of glass."

"Poor little cow," says Jenny, "now
I have to go. I'll come
back again, I promise,
and then I'll bring you some!

"Good night, you animals and dolls,
you flowers on the wall!
I'll come again, I don't know when,
and then I'll see you all!"

The morning sun spoils Jenny's fun.
It wakes her. No glass cow,
no dollhouse dolls call out to her,
the dream is over now—

But not forgotten. Jenny feels
a tingling in her toes.
That tingling *could*
    mean something good,
she might have grown, who knows?

That's right! She did grow in the night,
a tiny little bit!
Just enough so she can reach
the latch, and open it!

If Sarah knew, what would she do?
Whatever would she say?
She is at school from nine to noon,
she's safely far away.

Noon comes all too soon, and so
does Sarah: "You get out!
You're not allowed to be in here—"
Then Sarah looks about—

Surprise! She can't believe her eyes:
Nowhere a single trace
of any kind of messiness,
the toys are all in place,

The dollhouse neat and tidy,
the animals in rows.
(Jen arranged them carefully
while standing on her toes.

She also kept her promise to
the cow made out of glass:
She brought a tiny thimbleful
of garden-fresh green grass.)

No smudge, no smear, no mess in here!
Will sister Sarah say:
"Jenny, you are big enough
to play here any day—"?

Can you guess? The answer's yes!
But that is still not all:
Mother says that Jen can have
wallpaper on *her* wall!

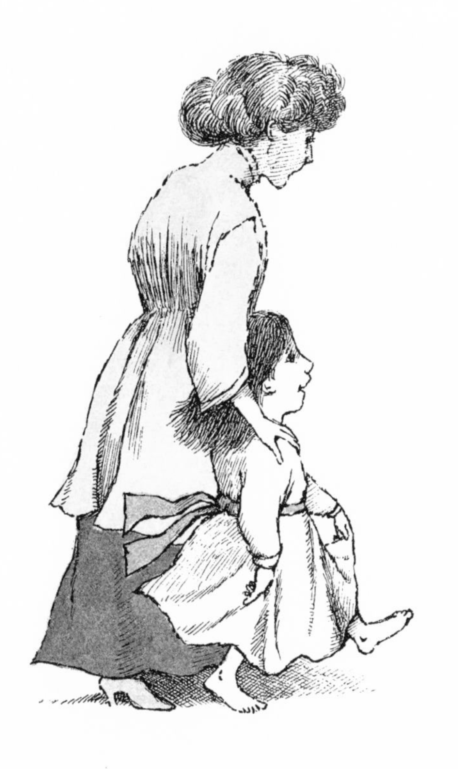

Now trees grow tall on Jenny's wall,
and morning glories bloom,
and she can use, as she may choose,
her own or Sarah's room!